CHEERFUL

CHEERFUL

A PICTURE-STORY

by

Palmer Brown

THE NEW YORK REVIEW
CHILDREN'S COLLECTION
New York

THIS IS A NEW YORK REVIEW BOOK
PUBLISHED BY THE NEW YORK
REVIEW OF BOOKS
435 Hudson Street, New York, NY 10014
www.nyrb.com

Published by arrangement with HarperCollins
Children's Books, a division of HarperCollins Publishers.

Library of Congress Cataloging-in-Publication Data
Brown, Palmer.
Cheerful / written and illustrated by Palmer Brown.
p. cm. — (New York Review Books children's
collection)
Summary: Cheerful, a city church mouse who dreams of
living in the country, sets off on an adventure.
ISBN 978-1-59017-501-9 (alk. paper)
[1. Mice—Fiction. 2. Adventure and adventurers—Fiction.
3. Country life—Fiction.] I. Title.
PZ7.B816647Ch 2012
[E]—dc23
                                        2012012239

ISBN 978-1-59017-501-9

Cover design by Louise Fili Ltd.

Printed in the United States of America on acid-free paper
1 3 5 7 9 10 8 6 4 2

CHEERFUL

CHEERFUL was a city mouse, raised in a church. His father came from a long line of sober black-whiskered churchmice, who made themselves useful by gathering rice scattered at weddings, or by picking up crumbs after church-ladies' cake sales and such delicious crumbs, too!

CHEERFUL'S mother was a light-footed woodmouse. She had come to the city quite by mistake, when she was packed up in a bundle of forest-scented spruce boughs, cut to festoon the church one Christmas. She soon found that no one knew the way back to the country again.

SO she made the best of it, and settled down to raise a family of four. There was Solemnity, who looked just like his father. There were Faith and Hope, who were almost as pretty as their mother, except that they did not have white feet, which are a nuisance in the city.

AST of all, there was Cheerful, who did have white feet, and long white whiskers too. Because his drooping whiskers made him look so sad when he was little, his mother said, "Be Cheerful!" And he tried to be, since that was his name. Most of the time it was easy.

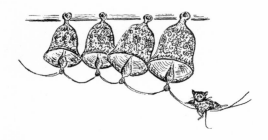

XCEPT on Sundays, Cheerful and his brother and sisters frisked for hours in the empty church, running races between the pews, or climbing the spiral stairs to the belfry. Sometimes, feeling very brave, they would tickle the whiskers of the sexton's cat, drowsing on the vestry steps.

BEST of all, they loved to play a special sort of tag, among the rainbow shadows streaming from the stained glass windows. Then Cheerful would rush to a patch of green shadow that was goal for him. He would sing:

Matthew, Mark, Luke, and John,
Guard the ground I stand upon!

THERE he was safe, and no one could tag him, for that was the rule. On rainy days, when no colored shadows fell, but only grey ones, Cheerful's mother would tell stories about the fields and woods where she once lived, far, far away. Sometimes she sang a lonesome song:

WHERE is that land
Where blue streams flow
Through golden sand,
    Now to, now fro?

Where winds of spring
    Stir fields aglow
With flowers that swing,
    So lazy, slow?

Where fairer skies
Than these I know
Greet hills that rise,
With clouds below?

You know the way?
Oh, tell me! Show
    The path today.
    Come, let us go!

HEERFUL wanted very much to go to that land, where spring was a sudden sweetness on the air, and winter a warm tunnel beneath the snow, where white feet never grew grey with city soot. But his mother did not know the way back. "That was so long ago," she said softly.

HEERFUL'S brother and sisters, not having white feet, did not worry about sooty paw pads. Faith grew up and married a mouse who lived in a bakery to one side of the church, and she grew fat on fancy crumbs of pies and cakes and cookies and cream-filled almond meringues.

HOPE grew up and married a mouse who lived in a delicatessen on the other side of the church. She too grew fat on smoked sausages and pickled fish and a dozen sorts of cheeses and biscuits. Cheerful hardly knew her when he went to visit her and see her well-fed family.

XANNAX

Little Licorice Lozeng

Particularly recommended for
soothing and salubrious vocal lubrication for
orators, preachers, actors, teachers, and
all other persons who most rely upon their
vocal chords in all sorts of ways, either
including operatic singers, birds. Also,
useful for all sudden emergency safe how
Contains sugar, glucose, licorice, brown
[illegible text]

SOLEMNITY, who resembled his father, decided to become a churchmouse too. Day by day he grew more and more solemn. He no longer played games, but took to nibbling the parson's licorice lozenges, which were kept in a little box behind the pulpit, and tasted very solemn.

OST of the time, then, Cheerful sat alone in his favorite green shadow, pretending it was a green field, and wishing that it were. And one day, when an open window called, he decided to leave home. So he kissed his mother good-bye, and he climbed to the stone window sill.

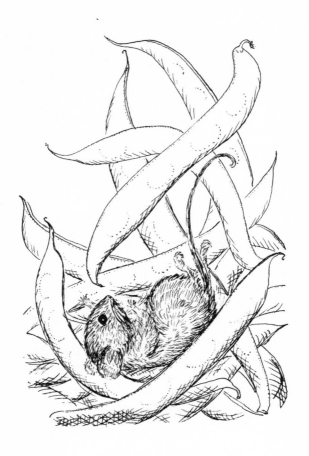

FF the ledge he hopped, into a pushcart below, full of fruits and vegetables. "Hide among the grapes, Cheerful!" his mother called. "They cost more, and should take you to a better home than those string beans." And it was true, the purple grapes did smell gloriously expensive.

SOON an old grandmother asked the pushcart man for grapes. Cheerful wriggled as far as he could into the biggest bunch, hanging on tight, and hoping that his tail would not show. The old lady bought the grapes, and Cheerful went home with her, deep inside a brown paper bag.

HEN the bag was opened, Cheerful was in the grandmother's kitchen, in a tall building in the city, where she lived alone with a cat named Daisy. Under a cupboard Cheerful made himself a bed in a cupcake paper, with a scrap of flowered calico for a coverlet to keep him warm.

THERE were dozens of good things to eat, because the grandmother did not believe in cleaning up and putting everything away all the time. Even when she took Daisy to visit her grand-daughter, Cheerful could always get along on pink peppermint pastilles, kept on the mantel.

YET Cheerful was not really happy there. He longed for a place where spring was more than just a potted cineraria on the window sill, and winter more than just a rumbling in the radiator pipes. He still yearned for the wonderful green land his mother had told him about.

E would watch the dusty sparrows fluff their feathers on the icy sill, and once he sang to them his mother's song, "Where is that land?" But the sparrows were city birds. They did not know the way, and they laughed at Cheerful's singing and made him feel foolish.

THE SECRET OF LIFE
IS
IN THE SEASONING

NE day, when kites were dancing over the treeless park below, the grand-mother came home from shopping, and she unwrapped gifts she had bought her grand-daughter for Easter. When she went to look for a packing box, Cheerful climbed onto the kitchen table to investigate.

FIRST he saw a pink-billed yellow bird, perched on a bright basket. Cheerful knew it was much too clean to be a city bird, so he sang his song, "Where is that land?" But the bird was only a paper finch, made of paint and wires and gilded tinsel. It could not answer him.

EXT he found a smiling rabbit, sprigged with blue forget-me-nots. Cheerful stood on tiptoe before the rabbit, singing his song into the rabbit's pink ears. But the rabbit was made of chocolate and spun sugar, and its heart was hollow. So it could not answer him either.

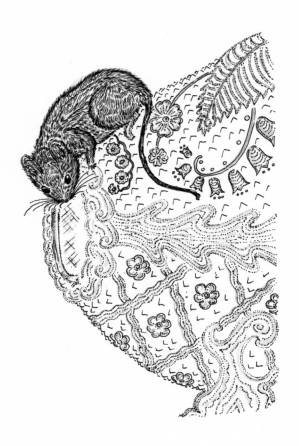

INALLY Cheerful saw a glorious egg of crystal sugar, crusted with flowers, and he peered in the round glass window. There he saw a lovely land, like that which he had dreamed of, with hills and streams, and meadows full of lambs! Again and again he rapped at the little window. No one came.

UICKLY he hopped on top of the egg. He tugged at a sugar rose, and it came loose, and he slipped inside. But all the lambs were made of sugar too, and all the hills were only frosted paper. Cheerful sat on a marzipan mushroom and wept. The tears were very sticky under foot.

UST then the grandmother came back with her packing box. She found the broken sugar rose, and she glued it back with boiled honey, so it was good as new. Then she put all her gifts in the box, and she tied it and mailed it to her granddaughter, who lived miles away.

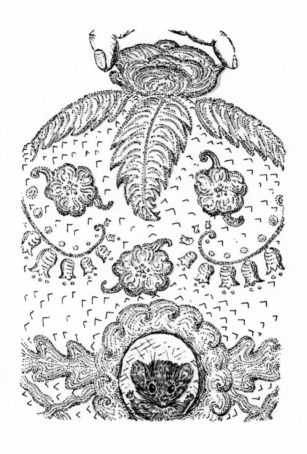

STILL inside the egg, Cheerful could not be cheerful at all. It was dark and stuffy, and when he got hungry, the rock candy was dusty and hard on the teeth. So he sang:

Matthew, Mark, Luke, and John,
Guard the ground I stand upon!

Then, even in the dark, he felt safe,
and he fell asleep.

WHEN he awoke, it was daylight, and a little girl was peeking in at him. She was so surprised to see him that she set the egg back on the grass, where it had been hidden for her, and she ran to tell her mother. And the egg rolled on its side, snapping off again the sugar rose.

S the egg turned over, Cheerful grasped at a crystal violet and tumbled through the hole. Without looking where he was going, he fled as fast and as far as he could. It was a long time before he stopped, or noticed that the wet grass had washed his white feet clean.

E stood deep in a spring-time meadow on the morning side of a hill, and a blue stream sparkled by. From the meadow a hundred voices sang, "We know the way!" From the forest a dozen breezes called, "This is the land!"

S Cheerful listened, a light-footed woodmouse came skipping through buttercups to greet him and ask him his name. Bowing whisker-low to offer her the crystal violet, he answered, "I am Cheerful." And, Oh! at last he was—to the very tip of his tail!

PALMER BROWN (1919–2012) was born in Chicago and attended Swarthmore and the University of Pennsylvania. He was the author and illustrator of five books for children: *Something for Christmas*; *Beyond the Pawpaw Trees* and its sequel, *The Silver Nutmeg*; *Cheerful*; and *Hickory*—all published by The New York Review Children's Collection.

E. NESBIT
The House of Arden

DANIEL PINKWATER
Lizard Music

ALASTAIR REID and BOB GILL
Supposing...

ALASTAIR REID and BEN SHAHN
Ounce Dice Trice

BARBARA SLEIGH
Carbonel and Calidor
Carbonel: The King of the Cats
The Kingdom of Carbonel

E. C. SPYKMAN
Terrible, Horrible Edie

FRANK TASHLIN
The Bear That Wasn't

JAMES THURBER
The 13 Clocks
The Wonderful O

ALISON UTTLEY
A Traveller in Time

T. H. WHITE
Mistress Masham's Repose

MARJORIE WINSLOW and ERIK BLEGVAD
Mud Pies and Other Recipes

REINER ZIMNIK
The Bear and the People